Estelle M. Hurll

Rembrandt

Estelle M. Hurll

Rembrandt

1st Edition | ISBN: 978-3-75236-672-3

Place of Publication: Frankfurt am Main, Germany

Year of Publication: 2020

Outlook Verlag GmbH, Germany.

REMBRANDT

BY

ESTELLE M. HURLL

INTRODUCTION

I. ON REMBRANDT'S CHARACTER AS AN ARTIST

A general impression prevails with the large picture-loving public that a special training is necessary to any proper appreciation of Rembrandt. He is the idol of the connoisseur because of his superb mastery of technique, his miracles of chiaroscuro, his blending of colors. Those who do not understand these matters must, it is supposed, stand quite without the pale of his admirers. Too many people, accepting this as a dictum, take no pains to make the acquaintance of the great Dutch master. It may be that they are repelled at the outset by Rembrandt's indifference to beauty. His pictures lack altogether those superficial qualities which to some are the first requisites of a picture. Weary of the familiar commonplaces of daily life, the popular imagination looks to art for happier scenes and fairer forms. This taste, so completely gratified by Raphael, is at first strangely disappointed by Rembrandt. While Raphael peoples his canvases with beautiful creatures of another realm, Rembrandt draws his material from the common world about us. In place of the fair women and charming children with whom Raphael delights us, he chooses his models from wrinkled old men and beggars. Rembrandt is nevertheless a poet and a visionary in his own way. "For physical beauty he substitutes moral expression," says Fromentin. If in the first glance at his picture we see only a transcript of common life, a second look discovers something in this common life that we have never before seen there. We look again, and we see behind the commonplace exterior the poetry of the inner life. A vision of the ideal hovers just beyond the real. Thus we gain refreshment, not by being lifted out of the world, but by a revelation of the beauty which is in the world. Rembrandt becomes to us henceforth an interpreter of the secrets of humanity. As Raphael has been surnamed "the divine," for the godlike beauty of his creations, so Rembrandt is "the human," for his sympathetic insight into the lives of his fellow men.

Even for those who are slow to catch the higher meaning of Rembrandt's work, there is still much to entertain and interest in his rare story-telling power—a gift which should in some measure compensate for his lack of superficial beauty. His story themes are almost exclusively Biblical, and his style is not less simple and direct than the narrative itself. Every detail counts for something in the development of the dramatic action. Probably no other artist has understood so well the pictorial qualities of patriarchal history. That singular union of poetry and prose, of mysticism and practical common sense, so striking in the Hebrew character, appealed powerfully to Rembrandt's imagination. It was peculiarly well represented in the scenes of angelic visitation. Jacob wrestling with the Angel affords a fine contrast between the strenuous realities of life and the pure white ideal rising majestically beyond. The homely group of Tobit's family is glorified by the light of the radiant angel soaring into heaven from the midst of them.

Rembrandt's New Testament scenes are equally well adapted to emphasize the eternal immanence of the supernatural in the natural. The Presentation in the Temple is invested with solemn significance; the simple Supper at Emmaus is raised into a sacrament by the transfigured countenance of the Christ. For all these contrasts between the actual and the ideal, Rembrandt had a perfect vehicle of artistic expression in chiaroscuro. In the mastery of the art of light and shade he is supreme. His entire artistic career was devoted to this great problem, and we can trace his success through all the great pictures from the Presentation to the Syndics.

Rembrandt apparently cared very little for the nude, for the delicate curves of the body and the exquisite colors of flesh. Yet to overbalance this disregard of beautiful form was his strong predilection for finery. None ever loved better the play of light upon jewels and satin `and armor, the rich effectiveness of Oriental stuffs and ecclesiastical vestments. Unable to gratify this taste in the portraits which he painted to order, he took every opportunity to paint both himself and his wife, Saskia, in costume. Wherever the subject admitted, he introduced what he could of rich detail. In the picture of Israel Blessing the Sons of Joseph, Asenath, as the wife of an Egyptian official, is appropriately adorned with jewels and finery. In the Sortie of the Civic Guard, Captain Cocq is resplendent in his military regalia.

With all this fondness for pretty things, Rembrandt never allowed his fancy to carry him beyond the limits of fitness in sacred art. The Venetian masters had represented the most solemn scenes of the New Testament with a pomp and magnificence entirely at variance with their meaning. Rembrandt understood better the real significance of Christianity, and made no such mistake. His Supper at Emmaus is the simple evening meal of three peasant pilgrims precisely as it is represented in the Gospel. His Christ Preaching includes a motley company of humble folk, such as the great Teacher loved to gather about him.

It was perhaps the obverse side of his fondness for finery, that Rembrandt had a strong leaning towards the picturesqueness of rags. A very interesting class of his etchings is devoted to genre studies and beggars. Here his disregard of the beautiful in the passion for expression reached an extreme. His subjects are often grotesque—sometimes repulsive—but always intensely human.

Reading human character with rare sympathy, he was profoundly touched by the poetry and the pathos of these miserable lives. Through all these studies runs a quaint vein of humor, relieving the pathos of the situations. The picturesque costume of the old Rat Killer tickles the sense of humor, and conveys somehow a delightful suggestion of his humbuggery which offsets the touching squalor of the grotesque little apprentice. And none but a humorist could have created the swaggering hostler's boy holding the Good Samaritan's horse.

As a revealer of character, Rembrandt reaches the climax of his power in his portraits. From this class of his pictures alone one can repeople Holland with the spirits of the seventeenth century. All classes and conditions and all ages came within the range of his magic brush and burin. The fresh girlhood of Saskia, the sturdy manhood of the Syndics, and the storied old age of his favorite old woman model show the scope of his power, and in Israel Blessing the Sons of Joseph he shows the whole range in a single composition. He is manifestly at his best when his sitter has pronounced features and wrinkled skin, a face full of character, which he understood so well how to depict. Obstacles stimulated him to his highest endeavor. Given the prosaic and hackneyed motif of the Syndics' composition, he rose to the highest point of artistic expression in a portrait group, in which a grand simplicity of technical style is united with a profound and intimate knowledge of human nature.

II. ON BOOKS OF REFERENCE

The history of modern Rembrandt bibliography properly begins with the famous work by C. Vosmaer, "Rembrandt Harmens van Rijn, sa Vie et ses Œuvres." Vosmaer profited by the researches of Kolloff and Burger to bring out a book which opened a new era in the appreciation of the great Dutch master. It was first issued in 1868, and was republished in 1877 in an enlarged edition. This book was practically alone in the field until the recent work of Emile Michel appeared. In the English translation (by Florence Simmonds) edited by Walter Armstrong, Michel's "Rembrandt" is at the present moment our standard authority on the subject. It is in two large illustrated volumes full of historical information and criticism and containing a complete classified list of Rembrandt's works—paintings, drawings, and etchings.

The "Complete Work of Rembrandt," by Wilhelm Bode, is now issuing from the press (1899), and will consist of eight volumes containing reproductions of all the master's pictures, with historical and descriptive text. It is to be hoped that this mammoth and costly work will be put into many large reference libraries, where students may consult it to see Rembrandt's work in its entirety.

The series of small German monographs edited by H. Knackfuss and now translated into English has one number devoted to Rembrandt, containing nearly one hundred and sixty reproductions from his works, with descriptive text. Kugler's "Handbook of the German, Flemish, and Dutch Schools," revised by J. A. Crowe, includes a brief account of Rembrandt's life and work, which may be taken as valuable and trustworthy. For a critical estimate of the character of Rembrandt's art, its strength and weaknesses, and its peculiarities, nothing can be more interesting than what Eugene Fromentin, French painter and critic, has written in his "Old Masters of Belgium and Holland."

Rembrandt's etchings have been the exclusive subject of many books. There are voluminous descriptive catalogues by Bartsch ("Le Peintre Graveur") Claussin, Wilson, Charles Blanc, Middleton, and Dutuit. A short monograph on "The Etchings of Rembrandt," by Philip Gilbert Hamerton (London, 1896), reviews the most famous prints in a very pleasant way.

There are valuable prints from the original plates of Rembrandt in the Harvey D. Parker collection of the Boston Museum of Fine Arts and in the Gray collection of the Fogg Museum at Cambridge, Massachusetts. Those who are not fortunate enough to have access to original prints will derive much satisfaction from the complete set of reproductions published in St. Petersburg (1890) with catalogue by Rovinski, and from the excellent reproductions of Amand Durand, Paris.

To come in touch with the spirit of the times and of the country of Rembrandt, the reader is referred to Motley's "Rise of the Dutch Republic," condensed and continued by W. E. Griffis.

III. HISTORICAL DIRECTORY OF THE PICTURES OF THIS COLLECTION

Portrait Frontispiece. National Gallery, London. Signed and dated 1640.

1. *Jacob Wrestling with the Angel*. Berlin Gallery. Signed and dated 1659. Figures life size. Size: 4 ft. 5-1/16 in. by 3 ft. 9-5/8 in.

2. *Israel Blessing the Sons of Joseph*. Cassel Gallery. Signed and dated 1656. Figures life size. Size: 5 ft. 8-9/16 in. by 6 ft. 6-3/4 in.

3. *The Angel Raphael Leaving the Family of Tobit*. Louvre, Paris. Signed and dated 1637. Size: 2 ft. 2-13/16 in. by 1 ft. 8-1/2 in.

4. *The Rat Killer*. Etching. Signed and dated 1632. Size: 5-1/2 in. by 4-9/16 in.

5. *The Philosopher in Meditation.* Louvre, Paris. Signed and dated 1633. Size: 11-7/16 in. by 13 in.

6. *The Good Samaritan.* Etching. Signed and dated 1633. Size: 10-1/5 in. by 8-3/5 in.

7. *The Presentation in the Temple.* At the Hague. Signed and dated 1631. Size: 2 ft. 4-11/16 in. by 1 ft. 6-7/8 in.

8. *Christ Preaching.* Etching. Date assigned by Michel, about 1652. Size: 6-1/5 in. by 8-1/5 in.

9. *Christ at Emmaus.* Louvre, Paris. Signed and dated 1648. Size: 2 ft. 2-13/16 in. by 2 ft. 1-5/8 in.

10. *Portrait of Saskia.* Cassel Gallery. Painted about 1632-1634. Life size. Size: 3 ft. 2-11/16 in. by 2 ft. 1-3/5 in.

11. *Sortie of the Civic Guard.* Ryks Museum (Trippenhuis), Amsterdam. Signed and dated 1642. Life size figures. Size: 11 ft. 9-3/8 in. by 14 ft. 3-5/16 in.

12. *Portrait of Jan Six.* Etching. Signed and dated 1647. Size: about 9-3/8 in. by 7-3/8 in.

13. *Portrait of an Old Woman.* Hermitage Gallery, St. Petersburg. Signed and dated 1654. Size: 3 ft. 6-7/8 in. by 2 ft. 9 in.

14. *The Syndics of the Cloth Guild.* Ryks Museum (Trippenhuis), Amsterdam. Signed and dated 1661. Life size figures. Size: 6 ft. 7/8 in. by 8 ft. 11-15/16 in.

15. *The Three Trees.* Etching, 1643. Size: 8-2/5 in. by 11 in.

IV. OUTLINE TABLE OF THE PRINCIPAL EVENTS IN REMBRANDT'S LIFE

1606.[1] Rembrandt born in Leyden.

1621. Rembrandt apprenticed to the painter, Jacob van Swanenburch.

1624. Rembrandt studied six months with Pieter Lastman in Amsterdam.

1627. Rembrandt's earliest known works, St. Paul in Prison, (Stuttgart Museum); The Money Changers (Berlin Gallery).

1631. Rembrandt removed to Amsterdam.

1631. The Presentation painted.

1632. The Anatomy Lecture painted.

1633. The portrait of the Shipbuilder and his Wife painted.

1634. Rembrandt married Saskia van Uylenborch, June 22, in Bildt.

1635. Rembrandt's son Rombertus baptized December 15. (Died in infancy.)

1637. Angel Raphael Leaving Family of Tobit painted.

1638. Rembrandt's daughter Cornelia born. (Died in early childhood.)

1639. Rembrandt bought a house in the Joden Breestraat.

1640. Rembrandt's second daughter born and died.

1640. Rembrandt's mother died.

1640. The Carpenter's Household painted.

1641. Manoah's Prayer painted.

1641. Rembrandt's son Titus baptized.

1642. Sortie of the Civic Guard (The Night Watch) painted for the hall of the Amsterdam Musketeers.

[1] Authorities are not entirely unanimous as to the date of Rembrandt's birth.

1642. Rembrandt's wife, Saskia, died.

1648. Christ at Emmaus painted.

1649. The Hundred Guilder print etched.

1651. Christ Appearing to Magdalen painted.

1652. Christ Preaching etched.

1656. Rembrandt's bankruptcy.

1656. Israel Blessing the Sons of Joseph painted.

1661. Portrait of the Syndics painted for the Guild of Drapers, Amsterdam.

1668. Rembrandt's son Titus died.

1669. Rembrandt died.

V. SOME OF REMBRANDT'S FAMOUS CONTEMPORARIES IN HOLLAND

Frederick Henry of Orange, stadtholder, 1625. Princess Amalia of Solms, wife of Frederick Henry, built the Huis ten Bosch (House in the Woods) at the Hague, 1647.

William II of Orange, stadtholder, 1647. In 1650 the stadt-holderate was suppressed, and John de Witt became in 1653 chief executive of the republic for twenty years. Murdered in 1672.

John of Barneveld, Grand Pensioner, "the greatest statesman in all the history of the Netherlands" (Griffis). Executed May 24, 1619.

Michael de Ruyter, "the Dutch Nelson," died 1676.

Marten Harpertzoon von Tromp, admiral. Born 1597; died 1691. (He defeated the English fleet under Blake.)

Cornelius Evertsen, admiral.

Floriszoon, admiral.

Witte de With, admiral.

Hendrik Hudson, navigator and discoverer; first voyage, 1607, last voyage, 1610.

Captain Zeachen, discoverer.

Hugo Grotius, father of international law, 1583-1645.

Jan Six, burgomaster, bibliophile, art connoisseur, and dramatist, 1618-1700.

Spinoza, philosopher, 1622-1677.

Joost van den Vondel, poet and dramatist, 1587-1679.

Jacob Cats, Grand Pensionary and poet, 1577-1660.

Constantine Huyghens, poet.

Gysbart Voet (Latin, Voetius) 1588-1678, professor of theology at Utrecht.

Cornelis Jansen, born 1585. Professor of scripture interpretation at Louvain.

Johannes Koch (Latin, Coccejus), 1603-1669, professor of theology at Leyden and, "after Erasmus, the father of modern Biblical criticism."

J. van Kampen, architect, built the Het Palais (Royal Palace) in Amsterdam, 1648.

Jansz Vinckenbrink, sculptor.

Hendrik de Keyser, sculptor.

Crabeth brothers, designers of stained glass.

Painters:—

Franz Hals, 1584-1666.

Gerard Honthorst, 1590-1656.

Albert Cuyp, 1605-1691.

Jan van Goyen, 1596-1656.

Jacob Ruysdael, 1625-1682.

Paul Potter, 1625-1654.

Jan Lievens, born 1607; died after 1672.

Salomon Koning, 1609-1668.

Gerard Terburg, 1608-1681.

Nicolas Berghem, 1620-1683.

Jan Steen, 1626-1679.

Adrian van Ostade, 1610-1685.

Rembrandt's pupils:—

Ferdinand Bol, 1616-1680.

Govert Flinck, 1615-1660.

Van den Eeckhont, 1620-1674.

Gerard Don, 1613-1680.

Nicolas Maes, 1632-1693.

Juriaen Ovens, 1623.

Hendrick Heerschop, born 1620, entered Rembrandt's studio, 1644.

Carl Fabritius, 1624-1654.

Samuel van Hoogstraaten, born 1627, with Rembrandt, 1640-1650.

Aert de Gelder, 1645-1727.

Less important names: Jan van Glabbeck, Jacobus Levecq, Heyman Dullaert, Johan Hendricksen, Adriaen Verdael, Cornelis Drost.

VI.   FOREIGN CONTEMPORARY PAINTERS

Flemish:—

Peter Paul Rubens, 1577-1640.

Anthony Van Dyck, 1599-1641.

Jacob Jordaens, 1594-1678.

Franz Snyders, 1574-1657.

Gaspard de Craeyer, 1582-1669.

David Teniers, 1610-1690.

Spanish:—

Velasquez, 1599-1660.

Pacheco, 1571-1654.

Cano, 1601-1676.

Herrera, 1576-1656.

Zurbaran, 1598-1662.

Murillo, 1618-1682.

French:—

Simon Vouet, 1582-1641.

Charles Le Brun, 1619-1690.

Eustache Le Sueur, 1617-1655.

Italian:—

Carlo Dolci, 1616-1686.

Guido Reni, 1575-1642.

Domenichino, 1581-1641.

Francesco Albani, 1578-1660.

Guercino, 1591-1666.

Sassoferrato, 1605-1685.

I

JACOB WRESTLING WITH THE ANGEL

The history of the Old Testament patriarch Jacob reads like a romance. He was the younger of the two sons of Isaac, and was at a great disadvantage on this account. Among his people the eldest son always became the family heir and also received the choicest blessing from the father, a privilege coveted as much as wealth. In this case therefore the privileged son was Jacob's brother Esau. Jacob resented keenly the inequality of his lot; and his mother sympathized with him, as he was her favorite. A feeling of enmity grew up between the brothers, and in the end Jacob did Esau a great wrong.

One day Esau came in from hunting, nearly starved, and finding his younger brother cooking some lentils, begged a portion of it for himself. Jacob seized the chance to make a sharp bargain. He offered his brother the food—which is called in the quaint Bible language a "mess of pottage"—making him promise in return that he would let their father give his blessing to the younger instead of the older son. Esau was a careless fellow, too hungry to think what he was saying, and so readily yielded.

But though Esau might sell his birthright in this fashion, the father would not have been willing to give the blessing to the younger son, had it not been for a trick planned by the mother. The old man was nearly blind, and knew his sons apart by the touch of their skin, as Esau had a rough, hairy skin and Jacob a smooth one. The mother put skins of kids upon Jacob's hands and neck and bade him go to his father pretending to be Esau, and seek his blessing. The trick was successful, and when a little later Esau himself came to his father on the same errand, he found that he had been superseded. Naturally he was very angry, and vowed vengeance on his brother. Jacob, fearing for his life, fled into a place called Padanaram.

In this place he became a prosperous cattle farmer and grew very rich. He married there also and had a large family of children. After fourteen years he bethought himself of his brother Esau and the great wrong he had done him. He resolved to remove his family to his old home, and to be reconciled with his brother. Hardly daring to expect to be favorably received, he sent in advance a large number of cattle in three droves as a gift to Esau. Then he awaited over night some news or message from his brother. In the night a strange adventure befell him. This is the way the story is told in the book of Genesis.[2]

[2] Genesis, chapter xxxii. verses 24-31.

JACOB WRESTLING WITH THE ANGEL
Berlin Gallery

Please click on the image for a larger image.

Please click here for a modern color image

"There wrestled a man with him until the breaking of the day. And when he saw that he prevailed not against him, he touched the hollow of his thigh; and the hollow of Jacob's thigh was out of joint, as he wrestled with him. And he said, 'Let me go, for the day breaketh.' And he said, 'I will not let thee go, except thou bless me,' And he said unto him, 'What is thy name?' And he said, 'Jacob,' And he said, 'Thy name shall be called no more Jacob, but Israel; for as a prince hast thou power with God and with men, and hast prevailed.'… And he blessed him there.

"And Jacob called the name of the place Peniel: for I have seen God face to face, and my life is preserved. And as he passed over Penuel, the sun rose upon him and he halted upon his thigh;" that is, he walked halt, or lame.

The crisis in Jacob's life was passed, for hardly had he set forth on this morning when he saw his brother whom he had wronged advancing with four

12

hundred men to meet him. "And Esau ran to meet him, and embraced him, and fell on his neck and kissed him: and they wept."

So were the brothers reconciled.

The picture represents Jacob wrestling with his mysterious adversary. We have seen from his history how determined he was to have his own way, and how he wrested worldly prosperity even from misfortunes. Now he is equally determined in this higher and more spiritual conflict. It is a very real struggle, and Jacob has prevailed only by putting forth his utmost energy. It is the moment when the grand angel, pressing one knee into the hollow of Jacob's left thigh and laying his hand on his right side, looks into his face and grants the blessing demanded as a condition for release. Strong and tender is his gaze, and the gift he bestows is a new name, in token of the new character of brotherly love of which this victory is the beginning.

The story of St. Michael and the Dragon, which Raphael has painted, stands for the everlasting conflict between good and evil in the world. There is a like meaning in the story of Jacob's wrestling with the angel. The struggle is in the human heart between selfish impulses and higher ideals. The day when one can hold on to the good angel long enough to win a blessing, is the day which begins a new chapter in a man's life.

II

ISRAEL BLESSING THE SONS OF JOSEPH

When Jacob wrestled with the angel he received a new name, Israel, or a prince, a champion of God.

Israel became the founder of the great Israelite nation, and from his twelve sons grew up the twelve tribes of Israel, among whom was distributed the country now called Palestine. Among these sons the father's favorite was Joseph, who was next to the youngest. This favoritism aroused the anger and jealousy of the older brothers, and they plotted to get rid of him. One day when they were all out with some flocks in a field quite distant from their home, they thought they were rid forever of the hated Joseph by selling him to a company of men who were journeying to Egypt. Then they dipped the lad's coat in goat's blood and carried it to Israel, who, supposing his son to have been devoured by a wild beast, mourned him as dead.

When Joseph had grown to manhood in Egypt, a singular chain of circumstances brought the brothers together again. There was a sore famine, and Egypt was the headquarters for the sale of corn. Joseph had shown himself so able and trustworthy that he was given charge of selling and distributing the stores of food. So when Israel's older sons came from their home to Egypt to buy corn they had to apply to Joseph, whom they little suspected of being the brother they had so cruelly wronged. There is a pretty story, too long to repeat here, of how Joseph disclosed himself to his astonished brethren, and forgave them their cruelty, how he sent for his father to come to Egypt to live near him, how there was a joyful reunion, and how "they all lived happily ever after."

When the time drew near for Israel to die, he desired to bestow his last blessing on his sons. And first of all his beloved son Joseph brought him his own two boys, Ephraim and Manasseh.

Now according to the traditions of the patriarchs, it was the eldest son who should receive the choicest blessing from his father. Israel, however, had found among his own sons that it was a younger one, Joseph, who had proved himself the most worthy of love. This may have shaken his faith in the wisdom of the old custom. Perhaps, too, he remembered how his own boyhood had been made unhappy because he was the younger son, and how he had on that account been tempted to deceit.

Whatever the reason, he surprised Joseph at the last moment by showing a preference for the younger of the two grandsons, Ephraim, expressing this preference by laying the right hand, instead of the left, on his head. The blessing was spoken in these solemn words: "God, before whom my fathers Abraham and Isaac did walk, the God which fed me all my life long unto this day, the Angel which redeemed me from all evil, bless the lads."

ISRAEL BLESSING THE SONS OF JOSEPH
Cassel Gallery

Please click on the image for a larger image.

Please click here for a modern color image

The narrative relates[3] that "When Joseph saw that his father laid his right hand upon the head of Ephraim, it displeased him; and he held up his father's hand, to remove it from Ephraim's head unto Manasseh's head. And Joseph said unto his father, 'Not so, my father: for this is the first-born; put thy right hand upon his head.' And his father refused, and said, 'I know it, my son, I know it: he also shall become a people, and he also shall be great; but truly his younger brother shall be greater than he, and his seed shall become a multitude of nations.' And he blessed them that day, saying, 'In thee shall Israel bless, saying, God make thee as Ephraim, and as Manasseh;' and he set Ephraim before Manasseh."

[3] Genesis, chapter xlviii. verses 17-20.

As we compare the picture with the story, it is easy to identify the figures. We are naturally interested in Joseph as the hero of so many romantic adventures. As a high Egyptian official, he makes a dignified appearance and wears a rich turban. His face is gentle and amiable, as we should expect of a loving son and forgiving brother.

In the old man we see the same Jacob who wrestled by night with the Angel and was redeemed from his life of selfishness. The same strong face is here, softened by sorrow and made tender by love. The years have cut deep lines of character in the forehead, and the flowing beard has become snowy white.

The dying patriarch has "strengthened himself," to sit up on the bed for his last duty, and his son Joseph supports him. The children kneel together by the bedside, the little Ephraim bending his fair head humbly to receive his grandfather's right hand, Manasseh looking up alertly, almost resentfully, as he sees that hand passing over his own head to his brother's. Joseph's wife Asenath, the children's mother, stands beyond, looking on musingly. We see that it is a moment of very solemn interest to all concerned. Though the patriarch's eyes are dim and his hand trembles, his old determined spirit makes itself manifest. Joseph is in perplexity between his filial respect and his solicitude for his first-born. He puts his fingers gently under his father's wrist, trying to lift the hand to the other head. The mother seems to smile as if well content. Perhaps she shares the grandfather's preference for little Ephraim.

The picture is a study in the three ages of man, childhood, manhood, and old age, brought together by the most tender and sacred ties of human life, in the circle of the family.

III

THE ANGEL RAPHAEL LEAVING THE FAMILY OF TOBIT

The story of Tobit is found in what is called the Apocrypha, that is, a collection of books written very much in the manner of the Bible, and formerly bound in Bibles between the Old and the New Testament.

The story goes that when Enemessar, King of Assyria, conquered the people of Israel, he led away many of them captive into Assyria, among them the family of Tobit, his wife Anna, and their son Tobias. They settled in Nineveh, and Tobit, being an honest man, was made purveyor to the king. That is, it was his business to provide food for the king's household.

In this office he was able to lay up a good deal of money, which he placed for safe keeping in the hands of Gabael, an Israelite who lived at Rages in Media. Tobit was a generous man, and he did many kind deeds for his less fortunate fellow exiles; he delighted in feeding the hungry and clothing the naked.

When Sennacherib was king of Assyria, many Jews were slain and left lying in the street, and Tobit, finding their neglected bodies, buried them secretly. One night, after some such deed of mercy, a sad affliction befell him. White films came over his eyes, causing total blindness. In his distress he prayed that he might die, and began to make preparations for death. He called his son Tobias to him and gave him much good advice as to his manner of life, and then desired him to go to Rages to obtain the money left there with Gabael. But Tobias must first seek a guide for the journey. "Therefore," says the story, "when he went to seek a man, he found Raphael that was an angel. But he knew not; and he said unto him, 'Canst thou go with me to Rages? and knowest thou those places well?' To whom the angel said, 'I will go with thee, and I know the way well: for I have lodged with our brother Gabael,'" The angel gave himself the name Azarias. "So they went forth both, and the young man's dog with them."

"As they went on their journey, they came in the evening to the river Tigris, and they lodged there. And when the young man went down to wash himself, a fish leaped out of the river, and would have devoured him. Then the angel said unto him, 'Take the fish,' And the young man laid hold of the fish, and drew it to land. To whom the angel said, 'Open the fish and take the gall, and put it up safely.' So the young man did as the angel commanded him, and when they had roasted the fish, they did eat it: then they both went on their way, till they drew near to Ecbatane. Then the young man said to the angel,

'Brother Azarias, to what use is the gall of the fish?' And he said unto him, 'It is good to anoint a man that hath whiteness in his eyes, and he shall be healed.'"

THE ANGEL RAPHAEL LEAVING THE FAMILY OF TOBIT
The Louvre, Paris

Please click on the image for a larger image.

Please click here for a modern color image

After this curious incident there were no further adventures till they came to Ecbatane. Here they lodged with Raguel, a kinsman of Tobit, and when Tobias saw Sara, the daughter, he loved her and determined to make her his wife. He therefore tarried fourteen days at Ecbatane, sending Azarias on to Rages for the money. This delay lengthened the time allotted for the journey, but at last the company drew near to Nineveh,—Azarias or Raphael, and Tobias, with the bride, the treasure, and the precious fishgall. Raphael then gave Tobias directions to use the gall for his father's eyes. Their arrival was the cause of great excitement. "Anna ran forth, and fell upon the neck of her son. Tobit also went forth toward the door, and stumbled: but his son ran unto him, and took hold of his father: and he strake of the gall on his father's eyes, saying, 'Be of good hope, my father.' And when his eyes began to smart, he rubbed them; and the whiteness pilled away from the corners of his eyes: and when he saw his son, he fell upon his neck."

Now Tobit and Tobias were full of gratitude to Azarias for all that he had done for them, and, consulting together as to how they could reward him, decided to give him half the treasure. So the old man called the angel, and said, "Take half of all that ye have brought, and go away in safety." Then Raphael took them both apart, and said unto them, "Bless God, praise him, and magnify him, and praise him for the things which he hath done unto you in the sight of all that live."

With this solemn introduction the angel goes on to tell Tobit that he had been with him when he had buried his dead countrymen, and that his good deeds were not hid from him, and that his prayers were remembered. He concludes by showing who he really is.

"I am Raphael, one of the seven holy angels, which present the prayers of the saints, and which go in and out before the glory of the Holy One."

"Then they were both troubled, and fell upon their faces: for they feared God. But he said unto them, 'Fear not, for it shall go well with you; praise God therefore. For not of any favor of mine, but by the will of our God I came; wherefore praise him for ever. All these days I did appear unto you; but I did neither eat nor drink, but ye did see a vision. Now therefore give God thanks: for I go up to him that sent me.'" "And when they arose, they saw him no more."

The picture shows us the moment when the angel suddenly rises from the midst of the little company and strikes out on his flight through the air like a strong swimmer. Tobit and Tobias fall on their knees without, while Anna and the bride Sara stand in the open door with the frightened little dog cowering beside them. The older people are overcome with wonder and awe, but Tobias and Sara, more bold, follow the radiant vision with rapturous gaze.

IV

THE RAT KILLER

The pictures we have examined thus far in this collection have been reproductions from Rembrandt's paintings. You will see at once that the picture of the Rat Killer is of another kind. The figures and objects are indicated by lines instead of by masses of color. You would call it a drawing, and it is in fact a drawing of one kind, but properly speaking, an etching. An etching is a drawing made on copper by means of a needle. The etcher first covers the surface of the metal with a layer of some waxy substance and draws his picture through this coating, or "etching ground," as it is called. Next he immerses the copper plate in an acid bath which "bites," or grooves, the metal along the lines he has drawn without affecting the parts protected by the etching ground.

The plate thus has a picture cut into its surface, and impressions of this picture may be taken by filling the lines with ink and pressing wet paper to the surface of the plate. You will notice that the difference between the work of an engraver and that of an etcher is that the former cuts the lines in his plate with engraving tools, while the latter only draws his picture on the plate and the acid cuts the lines. The word etching is derived from the Dutch *etzen*, and the most famous etchers in the world have been among Dutch and German artists.

THE RAT KILLER
Museum of Fine Arts, Boston

Please click on the image for a larger image.

Please click here for a modern image

Rembrandt is easily first of these, and we should have but a limited idea of his work if we did not examine some of his pictures of this kind. Impressions made directly from the original plates, over two centuries ago, are, of course, very rare and valuable, and are carefully preserved in the great libraries and museums of the world. There is a collection in the Museum of Fine Arts, Boston, where this etching of the Rat Killer may be seen.

The Rat Killer is one of many subjects from the scenes of common life which surrounded the artist. In smaller towns and villages, then as well as now, there were no large shops where goods were to be bought. Instead, all sorts of peddlers and traveling mechanics went from house to house—the knife grinder, the ragman, the fiddler, and many others. This picture of the Rat Killer suggests a very odd occupation. The pest of rats is, of course, much greater in old than in new countries. In Europe, and perhaps particularly in the northern countries of Holland and Germany, the old towns and villages have long been infested with these troublesome creatures.

There are some curious legends about them. One relates how a certain Bishop Hatto, as a judgment for his sins, was attacked by an army of rats which swam across the Rhine and invaded him in his island tower, where they made short work of their victim.[4] Another tells how a town called Hamelin was overrun with rats until a magic piper appeared who so charmed them with his enchanted music that they gathered about him and followed his leading till they came to the river and were drowned.[5]

[4] See Southey's poem, Bishop Hatto.

[5] See Browning's poem, The Pied Piper of Hamelin.

The old Rat Killer in the picture looks suspiciously like a magician. It seems as if he must have bewitched the rats which crawl friskily about him, one perching on his shoulders. He reminds one of some ogre out of a fairy tale, with his strange tall cap, his kilted coat, and baggy trousers, the money pouch at his belt, the fur mantle flung over one shoulder, and the fierce-looking sword dangling at his side. But there is no magic in his way of killing rats. He has some rat poison to sell which his apprentice, a miserable little creature, carries in a large box.

The picture gives us an idea of an old Dutch village street. The cottages are built very low, with steep overhanging roofs. The walls are of thick masonry, for these were days when in small villages and outlying districts "every man's house was his castle," that is, every man's house was intended, first of all, as a place of defense against outlawry.

The entrance doors were made in two sections, an upper and a lower part, or wing, each swinging on its own hinges. Whenever a knock came, the householder could open the upper wing and address the caller as through a window, first learning who he was and what his errand, before opening the lower part to admit him. Thus an unwelcome intruder could not press his way into the house by the door's being opened at his knock, and the family need not be taken unawares. In many of our modern houses we see doors made after the same plan, and known as "Dutch doors."

The cautious old man in the picture has no intention of being imposed upon by wandering fakirs. He has opened only the upper door and leans on the lower wing, as on a gate, while he listens to the Rat Killer's story. The latter must have a marvellous tale to tell of the effects of the poison, from the collection of dead rats which he carries as trophies in the basket fastened to the long pole in his hand. But the householder impatiently pushes his hand back, and turns away as if with disgust. The apprentice, grotesque little rat himself, looks up rather awestruck at this grand, turbaned figure above him.

V

THE PHILOSOPHER IN MEDITATION

Ever since the beginning of human history there have been people who puzzled their brains about the reasons of things. Why things are as they are, whence we came, and whither we are going are some of the perplexing questions they have tried to answer. Some men have given all their lives to the study of these problems as a single occupation or profession. Among the ancient Greeks, who were a very intellectual nation, such men were quite numerous and were held in great esteem as teachers. They were called philosophers, that is, lovers of wisdom, and this word has been passed down to our own times in various modern languages.

In the passing of the centuries men found more and more subjects to think about. Some studied the movements of the stars and tried to discover if they had any influence in human affairs. These men were called astrologers, and they drew plans, known as horoscopes, mapping out the future destiny of persons as revealed by the position of the constellations. There were other men who examined the various substances of which the earth is composed, putting them together to make new things. These were alchemists, and their great ambition was to find some preparation which would change baser metals into gold. This hoped-for preparation was spoken of as the "philosopher's stone."

Now modern learning has changed these vague experiments into exact science; astronomy has replaced astrology, and chemistry has taken the place of alchemy. Nevertheless these changes were brought about only very gradually, and in the 17th century, when Rembrandt lived and painted this picture, a great stir was made by the new ideas of astronomy taught by Galileo in Italy, and the new discoveries in chemistry made by Van Helmont in Belgium. Many philosophers still held to the old beliefs of astrology and alchemy.

It is not likely that Rembrandt had any one philosopher in mind as the subject of his picture. That his philosopher is something of a scholar, we judge from the table at which he sits, littered with writing materials. Yet he seems to care less for reading than for thinking, as he sits with hands clasped in his lap and his head sunk upon his breast. He wears a loose, flowing garment like a dressing-gown, and his bald head is protected by a small skull cap. His is an ideal place for a philosopher's musings. The walls are so thick that they shut out all the confusing noise of the world. A single window lets in light enough to read by through its many tiny panes. It is a bare little room, to be sure, with its ungarnished walls and stone-paved floor, but if a philosopher has the ordinary needs of life supplied he wants no luxuries. He asks for nothing more than quiet and uninterrupted leisure in which to pursue his meditations.

THE PHILOSOPHER IN MEDITATION
The Louvre, Paris

Please click on the image for a larger image.

Please click here for a modern color image

Our philosopher is well taken care of; for while his thoughts are on higher things and eternal truths, an old woman is busy at the fire in the corner. Evidently she looks after the material and temporal things of life. She kneels on the hearth and hangs a kettle over the cheerful blaze. The firelight glows on her face and gleams here and there on the brasses hanging in the chimney-piece above. Here is promise of something good to come, and when the philosopher is roused from his musings there will be a hot supper ready for him.

There are two mysteries in the room which arouse our curiosity. In the wall behind the philosopher's chair is a low, arched door heavily built with large hinges. Does this lead to some subterranean cavern, and what secret does it contain? Is it a laboratory where, with alembic and crucible, the philosopher searches the secrets of alchemy and tries to find the "philosopher's stone?" Is some hid treasure stored up there, as precious and as hard to reach as the hidden truths the philosopher tries to discover?

At the right side of the room a broad, winding staircase rises in large spirals and disappears in the gloom above. We follow it with wondering eyes which try to pierce the darkness and see whither it leads. Perhaps there is an upper chamber with windows open to the sky whence the philosopher studies the stars. This place with its winding staircase would be just such an observatory as an astrologer would like. Indeed it suggests at once the tower on the hillside near Florence where Galileo passed his declining years.

Our philosopher, too, is an old man; his hair has been whitened by many winters, his face traced over with many lines of thought. Even if his problems have not all been solved he has found rich satisfaction in his thinking; the end of his meditations is peace. The day is drawing to a close. The waning light falls through the window and illumines the philosopher's venerable face. It throws the upper spiral of the stairway into bold relief, and brings out all the beautiful curves in its structure. The bare little room is transfigured. This is indeed a fit dwelling-place for a philosopher whose thoughts, penetrating dark mysteries, are at last lighted by some gleams of the ideal.

VI

THE GOOD SAMARITAN

The story of the Good Samaritan was related by Jesus to a certain lawyer as a parable, that is, a story to teach a moral lesson. The object was to show what was true neighborly conduct; and this was the story:—[6]

"A certain man went down from Jerusalem to Jericho, and fell among thieves, which stripped him of his raiment, and wounded him, and departed, leaving him half dead. And by chance there came down a certain priest that way; and when he saw him, he passed by on the other side. And likewise a Levite, when he was at the place, came and looked on him, and passed by on the other side.

"But a certain Samaritan, as he journeyed, came where he was: and when he saw him, he had compassion on him, and went to him, and bound up his wounds, pouring in oil and wine, and set him on his own beast, and brought him to an inn, and took care of him. And on the morrow when he departed, he took out two pence, and gave them to the host, and said unto him, 'Take care of him; and whatsoever thou spendest more, when I come again I will repay thee.'"

[6] St. Luke, chapter x. verses 30-37.

The point of the story is very plain, and when Jesus asked the lawyer which one of the three passers-by was a neighbor to the wounded man, he was forced to reply, "He that shewed mercy." Then said Jesus simply, "Go, and do thou likewise."

Though the scene of the story is laid in Palestine, it is the sort of incident which one can imagine taking place in any country or period of time. So it seems perfectly proper that Rembrandt, in representing the subject, should show us an old Dutch scene. The etching illustrates that moment when the Good Samaritan arrives at the inn, followed by the wounded traveler mounted on his horse.

The building is a quaint piece of architecture with arched doors and windows. That it was built with an eye to possible attacks from thieves and outlaws, we may see from the small windows and thick walls of masonry, which make it look like a miniature fortress. This is a lonely spot, and inns are few and far between. The plaster is cracking and crumbling from the surface, and the whole appearance of the place does not betoken great thrift on the part of the owners. On the present occasion, during the working hours of the day, doors

26

and windows are open after the hospitable manner of an inn.

The host stands in the doorway, greeting the strangers, and the Good Samaritan is explaining the situation to him. In the mean time the inn servants have come forward: the hostler's boy holds the horse by the bridle, while a man lifts off the wounded traveler.

THE GOOD SAMARITAN
Museum of Fine Arts, Boston

Please click on the image for a larger image.

Please click here for a modern image

About the dooryard are the usual signs of life. In the rear a woman draws water from a well, lowering the bucket from the end of a long well-sweep, heedless of the stir about the door. Fowl scratch about in search of food, and there is a dog at one side. Some one within looks with idle curiosity from the window into the yard. It is little touches like these which give the scene such vividness and reality.

There is also a remarkable expressiveness in the figures which tells the story at a glance. You can see just what the Good Samaritan is saying, as he gestures with his left hand, and you can guess the inn-keeper's reply. Already he has put the proffered money into the wallet he carries at his belt, and listens attentively to the orders given him. He may privately wonder at his guest's singular kindness to a stranger, but with him business is business, and his place is to carry out his guest's wishes.

You see how the hostler's boy magnifies his office, swaggering with legs wide apart. Even the feather in his cap bristles with importance. This bit of comedy contrasts with the almost tragic expression of the wounded man. The stolid fellow who lifts him seems to hurt him very much, and he clasps his hands in an agony of pain. He seems to be telling the gentleman at the window of his recent misfortune.

To study the picture more critically, it will be interesting to notice how the important figures are massed together in the centre, and how the composition is built into a pyramid. Draw a line from the inn-keeper's head down the stairway at the left, and follow the outline of the Good Samaritan's right shoulder along the body of the wounded traveler, and you have the figure. This pyramidal form is emphasized again by the wainscot of the stairway at the left, and the well-sweep at the right.

To appreciate fully the character of the etching, one must examine attentively all the different kinds of lines which produce the varying effects of light and shadow. Below the picture Rembrandt wrote his name and the date 1633, with two Latin words meaning that he designed and etched the plate himself. This would seem to show that he was well pleased with his work, and it is interesting to learn that the great German poet, Goethe, admired the composition extravagantly.

VII

THE PRESENTATION IN THE TEMPLE

The story which the picture of the Presentation illustrates is a story of the infancy of Jesus Christ. According to the custom of the Jews at that time, every male child was "presented," or dedicated, to the Lord when about a month old. Jesus was born in Bethlehem of Judæa, a small town about four miles from the city of Jerusalem, the Jewish capital, where the temple was. When he was about a month old, his mother Mary and her husband Joseph, who were devout Jews, brought him to the great city for the ceremony of the presentation in the temple. Now the temple was a great place of worship where many religious ceremonies were taking place all the time.

Ordinarily, a party coming up from the country for some religious observance would not attract any special attention among the worshippers. But on the day when the infant Jesus was presented in the temple, a very strange thing occurred. The evangelist St. Luke[7] relates the circumstances.

[7] St. Luke, chapter ii. verses 25-35.

"And behold, there was a man in Jerusalem whose name was Simeon; and the same man was just and devout, waiting for the consolation of Israel: and the Holy Ghost was upon him. And it was revealed unto him by the Holy Ghost that he should not see death, before he had seen the Lord's Christ. And he came by the Spirit into the temple: and when the parents brought in the child Jesus, to do for him after the custom of the law, then took he him up in his arms, and blessed God, and said, Lord, now lettest thou thy servant depart in peace, according to thy word: for mine eyes have seen thy salvation which thou hast prepared before the face of all people, a light to lighten the Gentiles and the glory of thy people Israel.

THE PRESENTATION IN THE TEMPLE
The Hague Gallery

Please click on the image for a larger image.

Please click here for a modern color image

"And Joseph and his mother marveled at those things which were spoken of him. And Simeon blessed them, and said unto Mary his mother, Behold this child is set for the fall and rising again of many in Israel; and for a sign which shall be spoken against; that the thought of many hearts may be revealed."

In the picture we find ourselves, as it were, among the worshippers in the temple, looking at the group on the pavement in front of us—Mary and Joseph and Simeon, kneeling before a priest, with two or three onlookers. It is a Gothic cathedral, in whose dim recesses many people move hither and thither. At the right is a long flight of steps leading to a throne, which is overshadowed by a huge canopy. At the top of the steps we see the high priest seated with hands outstretched, receiving the people who throng up the stairway. It was towards this stairway that Mary and Joseph were making their way, when the aged Simeon first saw them, and recognized in the child they carried the one he had long expected. Taking the babe from his mother's arms, he kneels on the marble-tiled pavement and raises his face to heaven in thanksgiving. His embroidered cymar, or robe, falls about him in rich folds as he clasps his arms about the tiny swaddled figure.

Mary has dropped on her knees beside him, listening to his words with happy wonder. Joseph, just beyond, looks on with an expression of inquiry. He carries two turtle doves as the thank offering required of the mother by the religious law. His unkempt appearance and bare feet contrast with the neat dress of Mary. The tall priest standing before them extends his hands towards the group in a gesture of benediction. A broad ray of light gleams on his strange headdress, lights up his outstretched hand, and falls with dazzling brilliancy upon the soft round face of the babe, the smiling mother, and the venerable Simeon with flowing white hair and beard.

There are but few people to pay any heed to the strange incident. Two or three of those who climb the stairway turn about and stare curiously at the group below. There are three others still more interested. One man behind puts his turbaned head over Simeon's shoulders, peering inquisitively at the child, as if trying to see what the old man finds so remarkable in him. Beyond, two old beggars approach with a sort of good-natured interest. They are quaintly dressed, one of them wearing a very tall cap. Such humble folk as these alone seem to have time to notice others' affairs.

It must not be supposed that this scene very closely represents the actual event it illustrates. The painter Rembrandt knew nothing about the architecture of the old Jewish temple destroyed many centuries before. A Gothic cathedral was the finest house of worship known to him, so he thought out the scene as it would look in such surroundings. The people coming and going were such as he saw about him daily; the beggars looking at the Christ-child were the beggars of Amsterdam, and the men seated in the wooden settle at the right were like the respectable Dutch burghers of his acquaintance. It was like translating the story from Aramaic to Dutch, but in the process nothing is lost of its original touching beauty.

In studying the picture, you must notice how carefully all the figures are painted, even the very small ones in the darkest parts of the composition. The beautiful contrast, between the light on the central group and the soft dimness of the remoter parts of the cathedral, illustrates a style of work for which Rembrandt was very famous, and which we shall often see in his pictures.

VIII

CHRIST PREACHING

We read in the evangelists' record of the life of Jesus that he went about the country preaching the gospel (or the good news) of the kingdom of Heaven. Sometimes he preached in the synagogue on the Sabbath day; but more often he talked to the people in the open air, sometimes on the mountain-side, sometimes on the shore of the lake Gennesaret, or again in the streets of their towns.

The scribes and Pharisees were jealous of his popularity, and angry because he exposed their hypocrisy. The proud and rich found many of his sayings too hard to accept. So it was the poor and unhappy who were most eager to hear him, and they often formed a large part of his audience. Jesus himself rejoiced in this class of followers, and when John the Baptist's messengers came to him to inquire into his mission, he sent back the message, "The poor have the gospel preached to them."

In this picture of Christ Preaching, we see that his hearers are of just the kind that the preacher's message is intended for,—the weary and heavy-laden whom he called to himself. There are a few dignitaries in the gathering, it is true, standing pompously by in the hope of finding something to criticise. But Jesus pays no attention to them as he looks down into the faces of the listeners who most need his words. His pulpit is a square coping-stone in a courtyard, and the people gather about him in a circle in the positions most convenient to them.

CHRIST PREACHING
Museum of Fine Arts, Boston

Please click on the image for a larger image.

Please click here for a modern image

There is no formality here, no ceremony; each one may come and go as he pleases. Here is a mother sitting on the ground directly in front of the speaker, holding a babe in her arms, while a little fellow sprawls out on the ground beside her, drawing on the sand with his finger. Though we cannot see her face, we know that she is an absorbed listener, and Jesus seems to speak directly to her.

A pathetic-looking man beyond her is trying to take in the message in a wondering way, and a long-bearded man behind him is so aroused that he leans eagerly forward to catch every word. There are others, as is always the case, who listen very stolidly as if quite indifferent.

Again there are two who ponder the subject thoughtfully. One of these is in the rear,—a young man, perhaps one of Jesus' disciples; the other sits in front, crossing his legs, and supporting his chin with his hand. In the group at the right of Jesus we can easily pick out the scoffers and critics, listening intently, some of them more interested, perhaps, than they had expected to be.

As we look at Jesus himself, so gentle and tender, raising both hands as if to bless the company, we feel sure that he is speaking some message of comfort. One day when he was reading the Scriptures in the synagogue at Capernaum, he selected a passage which described his own work, and which perfectly applies to this picture. We can imagine that he is saying: "The spirit of the

Lord God is upon me; because the Lord hath anointed me to preach good tidings unto the meek; he hath sent me to bind up the brokenhearted, to proclaim liberty to the captives, and the opening of the prison to them that are bound; to proclaim the acceptable year of the Lord, and the day of vengeance of our God; to comfort all that mourn; to appoint unto them that mourn in Zion, to give unto them beauty for ashes, the oil of joy for mourning, the garment of praise for the spirit of heaviness."

It is a noticeable fact that the figures in this picture of Christ preaching are Dutch types. If you think that this is a strange way to illustrate scenes which took place in Palestine many centuries ago, you must remember that the picture was drawn by a Dutchman who knew nothing of Palestine, and indeed little of any country outside his own Holland. He wished to make the life of Christ seem real and vivid to his own countrymen; and the only way he could do this was to represent the scenes in the surroundings most familiar to himself and to them. The artist was simply trying to imagine what Jesus would do if he had come to Amsterdam in the seventeenth century, instead of to Jerusalem in the first century; somewhat as certain modern writers have tried to think what would take place "If Jesus came to Chicago," or "If Jesus came to Boston," in the nineteenth century. The sweet gentleness in the face of Christ and the eager attention of the people show how well Rembrandt understood the real meaning of the New Testament.

This picture is worthy of very special study because it is reckoned by critics one of the best of Rembrandt's etchings. One enthusiastic writer[8] says that "the full maturity of his genius is expressed in every feature." One must know a great deal about the technical processes of etching to appreciate fully all these excellencies; but even an inexperienced eye can see how few and simple are the lines which produce such striking effects of light and shadow: a scratch or two here, a few parallel lines drawn diagonally there; some coarse cross-hatching in one place, closer hatching in another; now and then a spot of the black ink itself,—and the whole scene is made alive, with Jesus standing in the midst, the light gleaming full upon his figure.

[8] Michel.

IX

CHRIST AT EMMAUS

The picture of Christ at Emmaus illustrates an event in the narrative of Christ's life which took place on the evening of the first Easter Sunday. It was now three days since the Crucifixion of Christ just outside Jerusalem, and the terrible scene was still very fresh in the minds of his disciples. It happened that late in the day two of them were going to a village called Emmaus, not very far from Jerusalem.

They made the journey on foot, and as they walked along the way, "they talked together," says the evangelist[9] who tells the story, "of all those things which had happened. And it came to pass, that, while they communed together and reasoned, Jesus himself drew near, and went with them. But their eyes were holden that they should not know him. And he said unto them, 'What manner of communications are these that ye have one to another, as ye walk, and are sad?' And the one of them, whose name was Cleopas, answering said unto him, 'Art thou only a stranger in Jerusalem, and hast not known the things which are come to pass there in these days?' And he said unto them, 'What things?' And they said unto him, 'Concerning Jesus of Nazareth.'" Then followed a conversation in which they told the stranger something of Jesus, and he in turn explained to them many things about the life and character of Jesus which they had never understood.

[9] St. Luke, chapter xxiv. verses 13-32.

"And they drew nigh unto the village, whither they went: and he made as though he would have gone further. But they constrained him, saying, 'Abide with us: for it is toward evening, and the day is far spent.' And he went in to tarry with them.

"And it came to pass, as he sat at meat with them, he took bread, and blessed it, and brake, and gave to them. And their eyes were opened and they knew him; and he vanished out of their sight. And they said one to another, 'Did not our hearts burn within us, while he talked with us by the way?'"

The picture suggests vividly to us that wonderful moment at Emmaus when the eyes of the disciples were opened, and they recognized their guest as Jesus, whom they had so recently seen crucified. The table is laid in a great bare room with the commonest furnishings, and the disciples appear to be laboring men, accustomed to "plain living and high thinking." They are coarsely dressed, and their feet are bare, as are also the feet of Jesus. One seems to have grasped the situation more quickly than the other, for he folds his hands together, reverently gazing directly into the face of Jesus. His companion, an older man, at the other end of the table, looks up astonished and mystified. The boy who is bringing food to the table is busy with his task, and does not notice any change in Jesus.

CHRIST AT EMMAUS
The Louvre, Paris

Please click on the image for a larger image.

Please click here for a modern color image

In the midst is Christ, "pale, emaciated, sitting facing us, breaking the bread as on the evening of the Last Supper, in his pilgrim robe, with his blackened lips, on which the torture has left its traces, his great brown eyes soft, widely opened, and raised towards heaven, with his cold nimbus, a sort of phosphorescence around him which envelops him in an indefinable glory, and that inexplicable look of a breathing human being who certainly has passed through death."

This description is by a celebrated French critic,[10] himself a painter, who knows whereof he speaks. He says that this picture alone is enough to establish the reputation of a man.

There is one artistic quality in the picture to which we must pay careful attention, as it is particularly characteristic of Rembrandt. This is the way in which the light and shadow are arranged, or what a critic would call the chiaroscuro of the picture. The heart of the composition glows with a golden light which comes from some unseen source. It falls on the white tablecloth with a dazzling brilliancy as if from some bright lamp. It gleams on the faces of the company, bringing out their expressions clearly. The arched recess behind the table is thrown into heavy shadow, against which the centrally lighted group is sharply contrasted.

This singular manner of bringing light and darkness into striking opposition makes the objects in a picture stand out very vividly. Some one has defined chiaroscuro as the "art of rendering the atmosphere visible and of painting an object enveloped in air." The art was carried to perfection by Rembrandt. You will notice it more or less in every picture of this collection, but nowhere is it more appropriate than here, where the appearance of Christ, as the source of light, emphasizes the mystery of the event and makes something sacred of this common scene.

As we compare this picture with the etching of Christ Preaching, we get a better idea of Rembrandt's aim in representing Christ. He did not try to make his face beautiful with regular classical features, after the manner of the old Italian painters. He did not even think it necessary to make his figure grand and imposing. Something still better Rembrandt sought to put into his picture, and this was a gentle expression of love.

X

PORTRAIT OF SASKIA

We should have but a very imperfect idea of Rembrandt's work if we did not learn something about the portraits he painted. It was for these that he was most esteemed in his own day, being the fashionable portrait painter of Amsterdam at a time when every person of means wished to have his likeness painted. A collection of his works of this kind would almost bring back again the citizens of Amsterdam in the seventeenth century, so life-like are these wonderful canvases. Among them we should find the various members of his family, his father and mother, his sister, his servant, his son, and most interesting of all, his beloved wife, Saskia.

Saskia was born in Friesland, one of nine children of a wealthy patrician family. Her father, Rombertus van Uylenborch, was a distinguished lawyer, who had had several important political missions intrusted to him. At one time he was sent as a messenger to William of Orange, and was sitting at table with that prince just before his assassination. He died in 1624, leaving Saskia an orphan, as she had lost her mother five years before. The little girl of twelve now began to live in turn with her married sisters. At the age of twenty she came to Amsterdam to live for a while with her cousin, the wife of a minister, Jan Cornelis Sylvius, whose face we know from one of Rembrandt's etchings. Saskia had also another cousin living in Amsterdam, Hendrick van Uylenborch, a man of artistic tastes, who had not succeeded as a painter, and had become a dealer in bric-à-brac and engravings. He was an old friend of Rembrandt; and when the young painter came to seek his fortune in the great city in 1631, he had made his home for a while with the art dealer.

It was doubtless Hendrick who introduced Rembrandt to Saskia. Probably the beginning of their acquaintance was through Rembrandt's painting Saskia's portrait in 1632. The relation between them soon grew quite friendly, for in the same year the young girl sat two or three times again to the painter. The friendship presently ended in courtship, and when Rembrandt pressed his suit the marriage seemed a very proper one. Saskia was of a fine family and had a sufficient dowry.

Rembrandt, though the son of a miller, was already a famous painter, much sought after for portraits, and with a promising career before him. The engagement was therefore approved by her guardians, but marriage being deferred till she came of age, the courtship lasted two happy years. During this time Rembrandt painted his lady love over and over again. It was one of his artistic methods to paint the same person many times. He was not one of the superficial painters who turn constantly from one model to another in search of new effects. He liked to make an exhaustive study of a single face in many moods, with many expressions and varied by different costumes.

PORTRAIT OF SASKIA
Cassel Gallery

Please click on the image for a larger image.

Please click here for a modern color image

Saskia had small eyes and a round nose, and was not at all beautiful according to classical standards. Rembrandt, however, cared less for beauty than for expression, and Saskia's face was very expressive, at times merry and almost roguish, and again quite serious. She had also a brilliant complexion and an abundance of silky hair, waving from her forehead. The painter had collected in his studio many pretty and fantastic things to use in his pictures,—velvets and gold embroidered cloaks, Oriental stuffs, laces, necklaces, and jewels. With these he loved to deck Saskia, heightening her girlish charms with the play of light upon these adornments.

One of the most famous of the many portraits of Saskia at this time is the picture we have here. Because it is not signed and dated, after Rembrandt's usual custom, it is thought that it was intended as a gift for Saskia herself, and thus it has a romantic interest for us. Also it is painted with extreme care, as the work of a lover offering the choicest fruit of his art.

The artist has arranged a picturesque costume for his sitter,—a broad-brimmed hat of red velvet with a sweeping white feather, an elaborate dress with embroidered yoke and full sleeves, a rich mantle draped over one shoulder, necklace, earrings, and bracelets of pearls. Her expression is more serious here than usual, though very happy, as if she was thinking of her lover; and in her hand she carries a sprig of rosemary, which in Holland is the symbol of betrothal, holding it near her heart.

The marriage finally took place in June, 1634, in the town of Bildt. The bridal pair then returned to Amsterdam to a happy home life. Rembrandt had no greater pleasure than in the quiet family circle, and Saskia had a simple loving nature, entirely devoted to her husband's happiness. A few years later Rembrandt moved into a fine house in the Breestraat, which he furnished richly with choice paintings and works of art.

A succession of portraits shows that the painter continued to paint his wife with loving pride. He represented her as a Jewish bride, as Flora, as an Odalisque, a Judith, a Susanna, and a Bathsheba. There is one painting of the husband and wife together, Saskia perched like a child on Rembrandt's knee, as he flourishes a wine-glass in the air. In another picture (an etching) they sit together at a table about the evening lamp, the wife with her needle-work, the artist with his engraving. The love between them is the brightest spot in Rembrandt's history, clouded as it was with many disappointments and troubles. As a celebrated writer has expressed it, Saskia was "a ray of sunshine in the perpetual chiaroscuro of his life."

XI

THE SORTIE OF THE CIVIC GUARD, OR THE NIGHT WATCH

The patriotism of the Dutch is seen through the entire history of "brave little Holland." Early in the sixteenth century every town of considerable size had a military company composed of the most prominent citizens. Each company, or guild, had a place of assembly, or *doelen*, and a drilling-ground. The officers were chosen for a year, and the highest appointments were those of captain, lieutenant, and ensign. Upon these civic guards rested the responsibility of maintaining the order and safety of the town. Sterner duties than these were theirs when in the late sixteenth century (1573), at the call of William of Orange, the various guilds formed themselves into volunteer companies to resist the Spanish. How well they acquitted themselves is a matter of history, and Spain recognized the republic in the treaty of 1609. After the war, many of the corporations were reorganized and continued to be of great importance in the seventeenth century.

The picture we have here represents the Civic Guard of Amsterdam during the captaincy of Frans Banning Cocq in 1642. Cocq was a man of wealth and influence who had purchased the estate of Purmerland in 1618 and had also been granted a patent of nobility. So it was natural that Lord Purmerland, one of the most distinguished citizens of the town, should be called to a term of office as captain of the Civic Guard. His magnificent stature and manly bearing show him well fitted for the honor.

SORTIE OF THE CIVIC GUARD
Ryks Museum, Amsterdam

Please click on the image for a larger image.

Please click here for a modern color image

The picture represents an occasion when the guard issues from the assembly hall, or doelen, in a sudden call to action. Captain Cocq leads the way with Lieutenant Willem van Ruytenberg, of Vlaerdingen, and as he advances gives orders to his fellow officer. The drum beats, the ensign unfurls the standard, every man carries a weapon of some sort. One is priming a musket, another loading his gun, another firing. A mass of lance-bearers press on from the rear. In the confusion a dog scampers into the midst and barks furiously at the drum. A little girl slips into the crowd on the other side, oddly out of place in such company, but quite fearless. It has been suggested that she may have been the bearer of the tidings which calls the guard forth. The quaint figure is clad in a long dress of some shimmering stuff, and she has the air of a small princess. From her belt hangs a cock, and she turns her face admiringly towards the great captain.

We do not know of any historical incident which precisely corresponds to the action in the picture. Indeed, it is not strictly speaking an historical picture at all, but rather a portrait group of the Civic Guard, in attitudes appropriate to their character as a military body. They may be going out for target practice or for a shooting match such as was held annually as a trial of skill; it may be a parade, or it may be, as some have fancied, a call to arms against a sudden attack from the enemy. In any case the noticeable thing is the readiness with which all respond to the call—the spirit of patriotism which animates the body. The Dutch are not naturally warlike, but rather a peace-loving people; lacking the quick impulsiveness of a more nervous race, they are of a somewhat heavy and deliberate temper; yet they have the solid worth which can be counted on in an emergency, and in love of country they are united to a man. Benjamin Franklin once said of Holland, "In love of liberty, and bravery in the defense of it, she has been our great example."

The picture cannot be fully understood without some knowledge of its history. Painted for the hall of the Amsterdam Musketeers, it was to take its place among others by contemporary painters, as a portrait group in honor of the officers of the year, and as a lasting memorial of their services. The other pictures had been stiff groups about a table, and the novelty of Rembrandt's composition displeased some of the members of the guild. Each person who figures in the scene had subscribed a certain sum towards the cost of the picture for his own portrait, and was anxious to get his money's worth. Consequently, there were many who did not at all relish their insignificance in the background, quite overshadowed by the glory of the captain and lieutenant. They thought they would have shown to much better advantage arranged in rows.

It was Rembrandt's way when painting a portrait to give life and reality to the figure, by showing the leading element in the character or occupation of the person. Thus his shipbuilder is designing a ship, the writing master, Coppenol, is mending a pen, the architect has his drawing utensils, and the preacher his Bible. So in the Civic Guard each man carries a weapon, and the figures are united in spirited action. All this artistic motive was lost upon those for whom the picture was painted, because of their petty vanity. So the great painting, now so highly esteemed, was not a success at the time.

In the following century it was removed to the town hall; and in order to fit it into a particular place on the wall, a strip was cut off each side the canvas. It is the loss of these margins which gives the composition the crowded appearance which so long seemed a strange fault in a great artist like Rembrandt.

The original colors of the painting grew so dark with the accumulation of smoke in the hall that the critics supposed the scene occurred at night, hence the incorrect name of the Night Watch was given to it. Since the picture was cleaned, in 1889, it is apparent that the incident occurred in the daytime, and if you look carefully you can plainly see the shadow of Captain Cocq's hand on the lieutenant's tunic.

XII

PORTRAIT OF JAN SIX

When the painter Rembrandt came to Amsterdam in 1631, a young man seeking his fortune in the great city, a lad of twelve years was living in his father's country seat, near by, who was later to become one of his warm friends. This was Jan Six, the subject of the portrait etching reproduced here. There was a great contrast in the circumstances of life in which the two friends grew up. Rembrandt was the son of a miller, and had his own way to make in the world. Jan Six was surrounded from his earliest years with everything which tended to the gratification of his natural taste for culture. Rembrandt's rare talent, however, overbalanced any lack of early advantages, and made him a friend worth having.

Six had come of Huguenot ancestry. His grandfather had fled to Holland during the Huguenot persecution in France, and had become a resident in Amsterdam in 1585. Jan's father, another Jan, had married a Dutch lady of good family, whose maiden name was Anna Wijmer. It was in the service of this good lady that we first hear of Rembrandt's connection with the Six family. He was called to paint her portrait in 1641, and must have then, if not before, made the acquaintance of her young son, Jan. Jan united to a great love of learning a love of everything beautiful, and was an ardent collector of objects of art. Paintings of the old Italian and early Dutch schools, rare prints and curios of various kinds, were his delight. He found in Rembrandt a man after his own heart. Already the painter had gone far beyond his means in filling his own house with costly works of art. So the two men, having a hobby in common, found a strong bond of union in their congenial tastes. We may be sure that they were often together, to show their new purchases and discuss their beauty.

PORTRAIT OF JAN SIX
Museum of Fine Arts, Boston

Please click on the image for a larger image.

Please click here for a modern image

Rembrandt, as an older and more experienced collector, would doubtless have good advice to offer his younger friend, and, an artist himself, would know how to judge correctly a work of art. One record of their friendship in these years is a little etched landscape which Rembrandt made in 1641, showing a bridge near the country estate of the Six family, a place called Elsbroek, near the village of Hillegom.

It was in 1647 that Rembrandt made this portrait of his friend, then twenty-nine years of age. Six had now begun to make a name for himself in the world of letters as a scholar and poet. He had already published a poem on Muiderberg (a village near Amsterdam), and by this time, doubtless, had under way his great literary work, the tragedy of Medæa. Many were the times when Rembrandt, coming to his house to talk over some new treasure-trove, found him in his library with his head buried in a book, and his thoughts far away. It was in such a moment that he must have had the idea of this beautiful portrait. He catches his friend one day in the corner of his library, standing with his back to the window to get the light on the book he is reading. He transfers the picture to a copper plate and hands it down to future generations.

The slender figure of the young man is clad in the picturesque dress of a gentleman of his time, with knee-breeches and low shoes, with wide white collar and cuffs. His abundant wavy blond hair falls to his shoulders; he has the air of a true poet. In his eagerness to read, he has flung his cavalier's cloak on the window seat behind him, a part of it dropping upon a chair beyond. Its voluminous folds make a cushion for him, as he leans gracefully against the window ledge. His sword and belt lie on the chair with the cloak. For the moment the pen is mightier than the sword. The furnishings of the room show the owner's tastes; a pile of folio volumes fill a low chair, an antique picture hangs on the wall.

The young man's face is seen by the light reflected from the pages of his open book. It is a refined, sensitive face, of high intellectual cast, amiable withal, and full of imagination. He is completely absorbed in his reading, a smile playing about his mouth. How little of a fop and how much of a poet he is, we see from his disordered collar. Breathing quickly as he bends over his book, in his excitement he cannot endure the restraint of a close collar. He has unloosed it, as, quite oblivious of any untidiness in his appearance, he hurries on, ruthlessly crushing the pages of the folio back, as he grasps it in his hand.

The friendship between Six and Rembrandt seemed to grow apace; for when the tragedy of Medæa was published, in 1648, it was illustrated by a magnificent etching by Rembrandt, representing the Marriage of Jason and Creusa.

The literary work of Jan Six led the way to various public honors. In 1656 he became commissioner of marriages; in 1667, a member of the Council of the States General of Holland, and in 1691, burgomaster of Amsterdam. His continued friendship for Rembrandt was shown in his purchasing a number of the latter's paintings. Rembrandt at length painted a magnificent portrait of his friend in his old age, which, with the portrait of his mother and the original plate for this etching, still remains in the Six family in Amsterdam. Referring to the portrait of Jan Six, the famous Dutch poet, Vondel, contemporary of Rembrandt and Six, paid a fitting tribute to the great burgomaster, as a "lover of science, art, and virtue."

XIII

PORTRAIT OF AN OLD WOMAN

The story is told of a little child who, upon being introduced to a kind-faced lady, looked up brightly into her eyes with the question, "Whose mother are you?" When we look into the wrinkled old face of this picture, the same sort of a question springs to mind, and we involuntarily ask, "Whose grandmother are you?" We are sure that children and grandchildren have leaned upon that capacious lap. The name of the subject is not known, though the same face appears many times in Rembrandt's works. But there are many people whose names we can quote, of whom we know much less than of this old woman.

The story of her life is written in the picture. Those clasped hands, large and knotted, have done much hard work. They have ministered to the needs of two generations. They have dandled the baby on her knee, and supported the little toddler taking his first steps. They have tended the child and wrought for the youth. They have built the fire on the hearth and swept out the house; they have kneaded the bread and filled the kettle; they have spun and woven, and sewed and mended. They have not even shrunk from the coarser labors of dooryard and field, the care of the cattle, the planting and harvesting. But labor has done nothing to coarsen the innate refinement of the soul which looks out of the fine old face.

She is resting now. The children and grandchildren have grown up to take care of themselves and their grandmother also. She has time to sit down in the twilight of life, just as she used to sit down at the close of each day's work, to think over what has happened. She has a large comfortable chair, and she is neatly dressed, as befits an old woman whose life work is done. A white kerchief is folded across her bosom, a shawl is wrapped about her shoulders, and a hood droops over her forehead. Her thoughts are far away from her present surroundings; something sad occupies them. She dreams of the past and perhaps also of the future. Sorrow as well as work has had a large share in her life, but she has borne it all with patient resignation. She is not one to complain, and does not mean to trouble others with her sadness. But left all alone with her musings, a look of yearning comes into her eyes as for something beautiful and much loved, lost long ago.

Some painters have been at great pains to fashion a countenance sorrowful enough and patient enough to represent the subject of the Mater Dolorosa, that is, the Sorrowing Mother of Christ. Perhaps they would have succeeded better if they had turned away from their own imaginations to some mother in real life, who has loved and worked and suffered like this one. The face answers in part our first question. A woman like this is capable of mothering great sons. Industrious, patient, self-sacrificing, she would spare herself nothing to train them faithfully. And the life of which her face speaks—a life of self-denying toil, ennobled by high ideals of duty—is the stuff of which heroes are made. Some of the great men of history had such mothers.

PORTRAIT OF AN OLD WOMAN
Hermitage Gallery, St. Petersburg

Please click on the image for a larger image.

Please click here for a modern color image

The picture illustrates the fact that a face may be interesting and even artistic, if not beautiful. This idea may surprise many, for when one calls a person "as pretty as a picture," it seems to be understood that it is only pretty people who make suitable models for pictures. Rembrandt, however, was of quite another mind. He was a student of character as well as a painter, and he cared to paint faces more for their expression than for beauty of feature.

Now the expression of a face is to a great extent the index of character. We say that the child has "no character in his face," meaning that his skin is still fair and smooth, before his thoughts and feelings have made any record there. Gradually the character impresses itself on his face. Experience acts almost like a sculptor's chisel, carving lines of care and grooving furrows of sorrow, shaping the mouth and the setting of the eyes.

The longer this process continues, the more expressive the face becomes, so that it is the old whose faces tell the most interesting stories of life. Rembrandt understood this perfectly, and none ever succeeded better than he in revealing the poetry and beauty of old age.

His way of showing the character in the face of this old woman is very common with him. The high light of the picture is concentrated on the face and is continued down upon the snowy kerchief. This forms a diamond of light shading by gradations into darker tints. It was the skillful use of light and shadow in the picture, which made a poetic and artistic work of a subject which another painter might have made very commonplace.

XIV

THE SYNDICS OF THE CLOTH GUILD

The word syndic is a name applied to an officer of a corporation, and this is its meaning in the title of the picture, The Syndics of the Cloth Guild. In Holland, as in England and France and elsewhere in Europe, guilds were associations of tradesmen or artisans united for purposes of mutual help and for the interests of their respective industries. In some points they were the forerunners of modern trades unions, except that the members were proprietary merchants and master craftsmen instead of employees, and their purpose was the advancement of commercial interests in municipal affairs, instead of the protection of labor against capital. There were guilds of mercers, wine merchants, goldsmiths, painters and many others.

Now the wool industry was one of the most important in Holland, hence the Guild of Drapers or Cloth Workers was a dignified association in several cities. There was one in Leyden, where Rembrandt was born, and another in Amsterdam, where he passed the most of his life. Amsterdam was at that time the foremost commercial city of Europe. Its guilds had fine halls, ornamented with works of art painted by the best contemporary artists. It was for this purpose that Rembrandt received from the Amsterdam Cloth Guild the commission to paint a portrait group of their five officers, and he accordingly delivered to them in 1661 the great picture of which we have this little reproduction to examine.

Just as in the picture of the Civic Guard he had given life to the portraits, by showing the members in some action appropriate to their military character, so here he represents the officers of the guild in surroundings suggestive of their duties. They are gathered about a table covered with a rich scarlet cloth, on which rests the great ledger of the corporation. They are engaged in balancing their accounts and preparing a report for the year, and a servant awaits their order in the rear of the apartment. Their task seems a pleasant one, for whatever difficulties have arisen during their administration, it is evident that the outcome is successful. They take a quiet satisfaction in the year's record.

It is as if in the midst of their consultations, as they turn the leaves of the ledger, we suddenly open the door into the room. They are surprised but not disturbed by the intrusion, and look genially towards the newcomers. The younger man at the end welcomes us with a smile. Next to him is one who has been leaning over the book. He raises his head and meets our eyes frankly and cordially. His companion continues his discourse, gesturing with the right hand. The older men at one side give more attention to the arrival. One seated in the armchair smiles good naturedly; the other, rising and leaning on the table, peers forward with a look of keen inquiry.

THE SYNDICS OF THE CLOTH GUILD
Ryks Museum, Amsterdam

Please click on the image for a larger image.

Please click here for a modern color image

As we examine the faces one by one, we could almost write a character study of each man, so wonderfully does the portrait reveal the inner life—the placid amiability of one, the quiet humor of another, the keen, incisive insight of a third. That they are all men of sound judgment we may well believe, and they are plainly men to be trusted. The motto of the guild is a key to their character: "Conform to your vows in all matters clearly within their jurisdiction; live honestly; be not influenced in your judgments by favor, hatred, or personal interest." These principles are at the foundation of the commercial prosperity for which Holland is noted.

The picture may be taken to illustrate a page in American history. It was the Dutch, as we all remember, who founded the State of New York, and the fifty years of their occupation (1614-1664) fell within the lifetime of Rembrandt. The fifteen thousand settlers, who came during this time from Holland to America, brought with them the manners and customs of their home country. The citizens of New Amsterdam were the counterparts of their contemporaries in the old Amsterdam. We may see, then, in this picture of the Cloth Merchants of Amsterdam just such men as were to be seen among our own colonists. In the broad-brimmed hat and the wide white collar we find the same peculiarities of dress, and in their honest faces we read the same national traits. It was to men like these that we owe a debt of gratitude for some of the best elements in our national life. In the words of a historian,[11] "The republican Dutchmen gave New York its tolerant and cosmopolitan character, insured its commercial supremacy, introduced the common schools, founded the oldest day school and the first Protestant church in the United States, and were pioneers in most of the ideas and institutions we boast of as distinctly American."

[11] W. E. Griffis, in *Brave Little Holland*, pp. 212-213.

If you fancy that it was quite accidental that the six figures of this picture are so well arranged, and wonder why the art of Rembrandt should be so praised here, you may try an experiment with your camera upon a group of six figures. In posing six persons in any order which is not stiff, and getting them all to look with one accord and quite naturally towards a single point, you will understand some of the many difficulties which Rembrandt overcame so simply.

XV

THE THREE TREES

Holland, as is well known, is a country built upon marshes, which have been drained and filled in by the patient industry of many generations of workers. The land is consequently very low, almost perfectly level, and is covered by a network of canals. It lacks many of the features which make up the natural scenery of other countries,—mountains and ravines, rocks and rivers,—but it is, nevertheless, a very picturesque country. Artists love it for the quiet beauty of its landscape. Though this is not grand and awe-inspiring, it is restful and attractive.

We may well believe that the artistic nature of Rembrandt was sensitive to the influences of his native Dutch scenery. Though his great forte in art lay in other directions, he paused from time to time to paint or etch a landscape.

Even in this unaccustomed work he proved himself a master. He treated the subject much as he did a portrait,—trying to bring out the character of the scene just as he brought out the character in a face. How much of a story he could tell in a single picture we see in this famous etching called The Three Trees.

One can tell at a glance that this is Holland. We look across a wide level stretch of land, and the eye travels on and on into an almost endless distance. Far away we see the windmills of a Dutch town outlined against the sky,—a sign of industry as important in Holland as are factory chimneys in some other parts of the world. Beyond this, another endless level stretch meets the sky at the horizon line. It is hard to distinguish the land and water, which seem to lie in alternate strips. The pastures are surrounded by canals as by fences.

THE THREE TREES
Museum of Fine Arts, Boston

Please click on the image for a larger image.

Please click here for a modern image

Here and there are cows grazing, and we are reminded of the fine dairy farms for which Holland is noted, the rich butter and cheese, which are the product of these vast flat lands, apparently so useless and unproductive. Directly in front of us, at the left, is a still pool, and on the farther bank stands a fisherman holding a rod over the water. A woman seated on the bank watches the process with intense interest. There are two other figures near by which can hardly be discerned.

The wide outlook of flat country is the setting for the little tree-crowned hill which rises near us at the right. It would seem a very small hillock anywhere else, but in these level surroundings it has a distinct character. It is the one striking feature which gives expression to the face of the landscape. The eye turns with pleasure to its grassy slopes and leafy trees. The trees have the symmetrical grace so characteristic of Dutch vegetation. Nothing is allowed to grow wild in this country. Every growing thing is carefully nurtured and trained. We see that the distances between these trees were carefully spaced in the planting, so that each one might develop independently and perfectly without injury to the others. The branches grow from their straight trunks at the same height, and they are plainly of the same age. Their outer branches interlace in brotherly companionship to make a solid leafy arbor, beneath which the wayfarer may find a shady retreat. On the summit of the hill, outlined against the sky, is a hay wagon followed by a man with a rake. At a

54

distance, also clearly seen against the sky, on the ridge of the hill, sits a man, alone and idle.

The sky is a wonderful part of the picture. Rembrandt, it appears, almost never ventured to represent the clouds. He had the true artist's reverence for subjects which were beyond his skill, and preferred to leave untouched what he could not do well. Now in this case, lacking the experience to draw a sky as finished in workmanship as his landscape, he *suggested* in a few lines the effect which he wished to produce. At the left a few diagonal strokes show a smart shower just at hand. A whirl of dark-colored clouds comes next, and in the upper air beyond, a stratum of clouds is indicated by a mass of lines crossing and recrossing in long swirling curves.

With these few lines Rembrandt conveys perfectly the idea that a storm is approaching. The clouds seem to be in motion, scurrying across the sky in advance of the rain. One imaginative critic has thought that he could discern in the cloud-whirl a dim phantom figure as of the spirit of the on-coming storm. Like the clouds we often see in nature, it takes some new fantastic shape every time we look at it. Altogether the impression we receive is that of vivid reality. The artist's few lines have produced with perfect success an effect, which might have been entirely spoiled had he tried to finish it carefully.

We look once more at the landscape to see what influence the coming storm has upon it. The fisherman pays no heed. The clouding of the sky only makes the fish bite better, and absorbed in his sport he cares nothing for weather. The haymaker on the hilltop has a better chance to read the face of the sky, and starts up his wagon. The three trees seem to feel the impending danger. Their leafage is already darkening in the changed light, and they toss their branches in the wind, as if to wrestle with the spirit of the storm.

XVI

THE PORTRAIT OF REMBRANDT

In studying the fifteen pictures of this collection, we have seen something of the work of the great Dutch master, Rembrandt, and have learned a little of the man himself, of his love for the sweet wife, Saskia, of his friendship with the cultured burgomaster, Jan Six, of his faithful and reverent study of the Bible, of his rare insight into people's character. We are ready now to look directly into the artist's own face, in a portrait by his own hand.

There are a great many portraits of Rembrandt etched and painted by himself. We have noticed how fond he was of painting the same model many times, in order to make a thorough study of the face, in varying moods and expressions. Now there was one sitter who was always at hand, and ready to do his bidding. He had only to take a position in front of a mirror, and there was this model willing to pose in any position and with any expression he desired. So obliging a sitter could nowhere else be found; and thus it is that there is such a large collection of his self-made portraits.

His habit of painting his own portrait gave him an opportunity to study all sorts of costume effects. His patrons were plain, slow-going Dutchmen who did not want any "fancy" effects in their portraits. They wished first of all a faithful likeness in such clothing as they ordinarily wore. It was chiefly in his own portraits that Rembrandt had the satisfaction of painting the rich and fanciful costumes he loved so well. He wore in turn all sorts of hats and caps, many jewels and ornaments, and every variety of mantle, doublet, and cuirass. In this he was somewhat like an actor taking the parts of many different characters. Sometimes he is an officer with mustaches fiercely twisted, carrying his head with a dashing military air. Again he is a cavalier wearing his velvet mantle, and plumed hat, with the languid elegance of a gentleman of leisure. Sometimes he seems a mere country boor, a rough, unkempt fellow, with coarse features and a heavy expression.

As we see him acting so many rôles, we may well wonder what the character of the man really was. As a matter of fact, he was full of singular contradictions. In his personal habits he was frugal and temperate to the last degree, preferring the simplest fare, and contenting himself with a lunch of herring and cheese when occupied with his work. On the other hand, his artistic tastes led him into reckless extravagance. He thought no price too great to pay for a choice painting, or rare print, upon which he had set his heart. He was generous to a fault, fond of his friends, yet living much alone.

In the portrait we have chosen for our frontispiece, we like to believe that we see Rembrandt, the man himself. He wears one of his rich studio costumes, but the face which he turns to ours is quite free from any affectation; a spirit of sincerity looks out of his kindly eyes. The portrait is signed and dated 1640, so that the man is between thirty and thirty-five years of age. This was the happiest period of Rembrandt's life, while his wife Saskia was still living to brighten his home.

We see his contentment in his face. He has large mobile features, which have here settled into an expression of genial repose. He has the dignified bearing of one whose professional success entitles him to a just sense of self-satisfaction, but he is not posing as a great man. He is still a simple-hearted miller's son, a man whom we should like to meet in his own family circle, with his little ones playing about him. He is a man to whom children might run, sure of a friendly welcome; he is a man whom strangers might trust, sure of his sincerity. It is, in short, Rembrandt, with all the kindliest human qualities uppermost, which show us, behind the artist, the man himself.

Lightning Source UK Ltd.
Milton Keynes UK
UKHW041841060820
367830UK00008B/1110